Daddy's Little Girl

by Allene van Oirschot

TATE PUBLISHING & *Enterprises*

This title is also available as a Tate Out Loud product. Visit www.tatepublishing.com for more information.

Published by Tate Publishing & Enterprises, LLC
127 E. Trade Center Terrace | Mustang, Oklahoma 73064 USA
1.888.361.9473 | www.tatepublishing.com

Tate Publishing is committed to excellence in the publishing industry. The company reflects the philosophy established by the founders, based on Psalm 68:11,
"The Lord gave the word and great was the company of those who published it."

Book design copyright © 2010 by Tate Publishing, LLC. All rights reserved.
Cover and interior design by Elizabeth A. Mason
Illustrations by Jason Hutton

Published in the United States of America

ISBN: 978-1-61663-106-2
1. Juvenile Fiction: Family: General
2. Juvenile Fiction: General
10.02.12

Dedication

For my little girls and boys: you are the best of me. For my husband, David: God blessed the broken road that led me to you, and I am grateful for his gift.

A daughter may
outgrow your lap,
but she will never
outgrow your heart.

~Author unknown

A father looked down into his newborn baby's eyes and stared at this new bundle of love. He barely knew this little person, yet she already held a place in his heart. He didn't think there was much room for anything else. He knew that this little baby would bring him nothing but joy.

"If only you could stay little forever,
I'd hold you in my arms, protect you from this world.
If only you could stay little forever,
you'd be by my side 'cause you're daddy's little girl."

He loved to watch her when she first started to crawl. She would make her way to the bottom of his chair and lift up her tiny arms to him. His heart would melt each time, and reaching down, he would whisk her up into an embrace. Then he would softly brush the little curls out of her eyes and whisper to her,

"If only you could stay little forever,
I'd hold you in my arms, protect you from this world.
If only you could stay little forever,
you'd be by my side 'cause you're daddy's little girl."

Well, time passed, and that little baby turned two. She loved to play with mommy's makeup and draw all over the walls. Filled with wonder and spirit, she learned to climb everything in sight. One day, she took a tumble, and her father ran to her cries. Quickly taking her in his arms, he gently rubbed her back and said,

"If only you could stay little forever,
I'd hold you in my arms, protect you from this world.
If only you could stay little forever,
you'd be by my side 'cause you're daddy's little girl."

Tomorrows soon became today, and the little girl was dressed for her first day of school. She stood with confidence and was filled with joy, backpack on and ready to take her first ride on the school bus. Her father took her hand and led her down the street. His grip was a little tighter today, and his heart was a little heavy. After helping her on the bus, he watched his big girl wave to him through the window. She raised her hand and touched it to her lips then blew kisses out the window. Her father reached out his arm, pretending to catch the kiss. Holding it tightly, he said,

"If only you could stay little forever,
I'd hold you in my arms, protect you from this world.
If only you could stay little forever,
you'd be by my side 'cause you're daddy's little girl."

Life blew by like a fierce wind, taking with it the little girl. She was always very busy with soccer, friends, and even boys. There was no more time for cuddles and kisses with her dad. But when she would go to bed and fall fast asleep, her father would look in on her and stare at his little girl all grown up, and his heart would ache.

Then he would bend down and softly press his lips to her curl-topped head and say,

"If only you could stay little forever,
I'd hold you in my arms, protect you from this world.
If only you could stay little forever,
you'd be by my side 'cause you're daddy's little girl."

Soon, school was in the past and years flew by too quickly. The young lady was now a woman and about to be wed. Her father stood near her side as she nervously waited to walk down the aisle. His heart was filled with mixed feelings. He was happy for her to have found love but was filled with great sadness that this woman was no longer his little baby girl. He softly brushed her cheek and blinked away his tears. Kissing her lightly, he said,

"I know you can't be little forever.
I can no longer protect you from this world.
I know you can't be little forever,
but you'll always be daddy's little girl."

e|LIVE

listen|imagine|view|experience

AUDIO BOOK DOWNLOAD INCLUDED WITH THIS BOOK!

In your hands you hold a complete digital entertainment package. In addition to the paper version, you receive a free download of the audio version of this book. Simply use the code listed below when visiting our website. Once downloaded to your computer, you can listen to the book through your computer's speakers, burn it to an audio CD or save the file to your portable music device (such as Apple's popular iPod) and listen on the go!

How to get your free audio book digital download:

1. Visit www.tatepublishing.com and click on the e|LIVE logo on the home page.
2. Enter the following coupon code:
   def9-c53f-8858-bde1-da77-1236-aa41-bd94
3. Download the audio book from your e|LIVE digital locker and begin enjoying your new digital entertainment package today!

Made in the USA
San Bernardino, CA
27 September 2016